MAGNUS MAXIMUS,
A MARVELOUS MEASURER

KATHLEEN T. PELLEY

PICTURES BY S. D. SCHINDLER

FARRAR STRAUS GIROUX

NEW YORK

There once was an old man who loved to measure things. His name was
Magnus Maximus, and he lived all alone in a ramshackle house in a town by
the sea. While other people there measured ordinary things like the width of a
waist, the height of a child, or the length of a foot, Magnus Maximus measured
more extraordinary things.

He filled his house with all kinds of clocks and scales, thermometers and barometers, and telescopes and periscopes. With his glasses perched at the end of his nose, he measured wetness and dryness, nearness and farness, and everything else in between.

"Magnus Maximus is a marvelous measurer," people said to one another.

As well as measuring, Magnus Maximus liked to count.

While other people counted ordinary things like pennies in a purse, buttons in a row, candles on a cake, stitches on a needle, or chocolates in a box,

Magnus Maximus counted more extraordinary things. He counted clouds in the sky, petals on a geranium, freckles on a nose, measles on a tummy, or raisins in a bun.

After Magnus had finished all his measuring and counting, he would write everything down on a piece of paper and paste it like a badge onto the tree trunk, or the donkey's ear, or whatever it was that he had measured. "It is good to know what's what, who's who, and the long and the short of a thing," he said.

Everyone agreed. "Magnus Maximus is really a marvelous measurer," they said.

One day, when a traveling circus
was passing through the town, a lion
escaped and paraded down High Street,
swishing his tail and tossing his mane from side
to side. People screamed and scrambled up lampposts.
They skittered and scattered. They flitted and fluttered
in a terrible dither.

But Magnus Maximus marched right up to that lion with his hand held high. "Halt!" he cried in a stern voice. Then he opened his bag and pulled out a tape measure and a stethoscope. "Sit still while I measure you," he scolded. So startled was the lion, that he did as he was told.

Magnus Maximus measured the length of his tail and the width of his whiskers.

He counted the number of fleas in his mane. And just as he had plugged in his stethoscope to count the number of beats in his heart, along came the trainer to take the lion away.

Word of Magnus and the lion spread from town to town. People marveled at his measuring. They had a statue of him made, and placed it outside the Town Hall. The mayor declared him to be the town's official measurer at a special ceremony with balloons, streamers, and a marching brass band. Even the queen came to snip the ribbon and give a speech. Folks cheered and clapped and cried, "Magnus Maximus! What a marvelous measurer!"

Now that he was the town's official measurer, Magnus Maximus had to measure all kinds of NESSes, from the wobbliness of a jellyfish to the itchiness of an itch.

Every Saturday morning in the town square,
he held a contest to measure all kinds of ESTs,

from the floppiest ears

to the stinkiest socks.

The problem with all this measuring was that Magnus Maximus forgot about everything else. Whenever he went for a walk, he was so busy counting the number of houses he passed, or the number of cracks in the sidewalk, that he never noticed the butterfly that danced by on apricot wings, or the blackbird that sang to him from the shade of an elm tree.

Whenever his friends invited him over to dinner, he was so busy counting the number of peas in the stew or cherries in the pie, that he never noticed the smiles in their eyes, or the tears in their voices.

Each night at bedtime, Magnus Maximus spent so much time counting the number of bubbles in his bath, bristles on his toothbrush, or stripes on his pajamas, that he fell asleep before he could say his prayers or count his blessings.

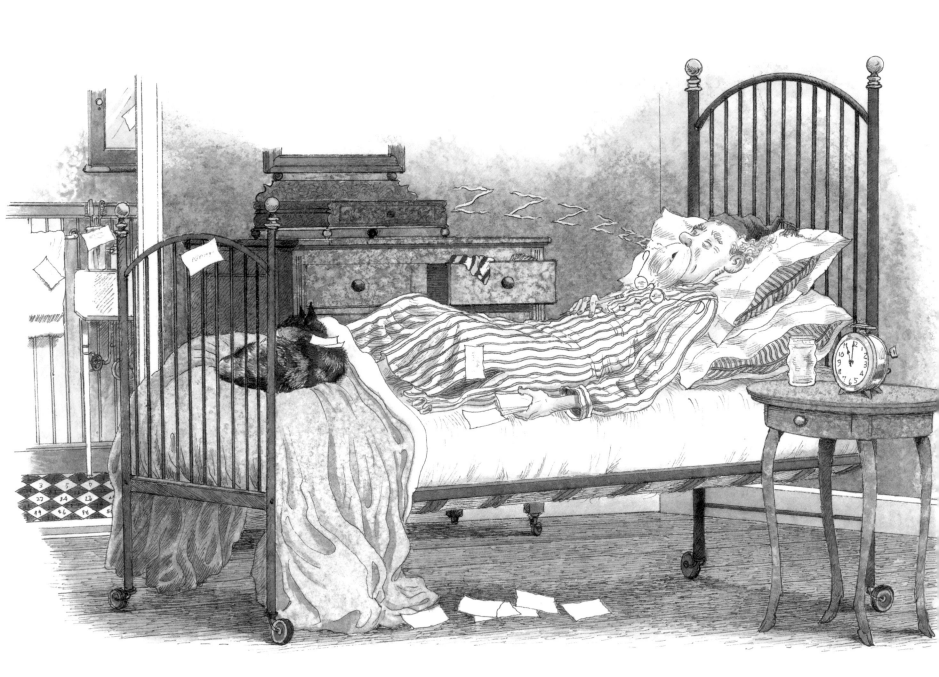

One morning, as Magnus Maximus stood in his kitchen counting the number of holes in a fishing net, he took off his glasses to rub his eyes. As he laid the glasses on the table behind him, up jumped his cat and knocked them to the floor. "Now where did my glasses go?" muttered Magnus Maximus as he took a step backward. *Crick, crack, crickle*—Magnus Maximus heard his glasses crunch beneath his foot. "Oh no!" he wailed. "Now I will have to go into town and buy a new pair."

At the eye doctor's office, the doctor told him, "I'm sorry, Mr. Maximus, but your new glasses will not be ready until tomorrow morning."

"Oh dear, whatever shall I do?" muttered Magnus Maximus. "I won't be able to measure anything now. Perhaps I could go down to the sea and count the waves."

So Magnus Maximus wandered down to the beach and sat on a rock. Just as he was beginning to count the rolling waves, he felt a tug at his sleeve. There stood a small boy with his hand outstretched.

Immediately Magnus Maximus reached into his pocket and pulled out his tape measure. Then with a frown and a shake of his head, he remembered. "Oh no, I'm sorry," he said, "I can't measure your hand without my glasses."

"But I don't want you to measure it, Mr. Maximus," said the boy.

Magnus Maximus scratched his head. "Well, what do you want me to do with it?" he asked.

"Why, hold it, of course," said the boy, whose name was Michael. "And come paddle in the waves with me."

Magnus Maximus blinked three times very quickly. Then he sighed—a long, slow sigh, like the sigh of the sea or the wind. "Oh, I see," he said with a small smile. And he reached out and took Michael's hand in his.

Together they walked down to the edge of the sea. They peeled off their shoes and socks and paddled in the water. Icy waves nibbled their toes as they shrieked and sang a silly song.

They built a sand castle with a moat and four turrets. And Magnus Maximus used his red-spotted hanky as a flag. At the end of the day, he waved goodbye to Michael and set off for home whistling a jaunty jig.

That night, Magnus Maximus forgot all about counting bubbles or bristles or stripes. Instead, he fell asleep, remembering the foamy white crests of the waves and the snugness of a hand in a hand.

The next morning, Magnus Maximus rushed into town to collect his new glasses. He went back home and began to measure as usual.

But that evening, as the clock in the hall chimed six, he put away his clocks and scales, his thermometers and barometers, his telescopes and periscopes, and he tucked his glasses into his pocket.

He made a pot of tea and a plate of sardine sandwiches, and he sat outside in his garden. Then Magnus Maximus, that most marvelous of measurers, crooned a lullaby to himself as he watched the sun set, the moon swell, and the stars speckle an endless sky.

To my husband, Chris, a most marvelous measurer —K.T.P.

To Richard: Keep on measurin' —S.D.S.

Text copyright © 2010 by Kathleen T. Pelley
Pictures copyright © 2010 by S. D. Schindler
Distributed in Canada by D&M Publishers, Inc.
Color separations by Embassy Graphics Ltd.
Printed in October 2009 in China by SNP Leefung Printers Ltd.,
Dongguan City, Guangdong Province
Designed by Jay Colvin
First edition, 2010
1   3   5   7   9   10   8   6   4   2

www.fsgkidsbooks.com

Library of Congress Cataloging-in-Publication Data
Pelley, Kathleen T.
    Magnus Maximus, a marvelous measurer / Kathleen T. Pelley ; pictures by S. D.
Schindler.— 1st ed.
        p.   cm.
    Summary: As the town's official measurer, Magnus Maximus is consumed with
measuring and counting everything and everyone, missing out on life's simple
pleasures, until one day when he breaks his glasses.
    ISBN: 978-0-374-34725-3
    [1. Measurement—Fiction.   2. Counting—Fiction.   3. Conduct of life—Fiction.]
I. Schindler, S. D., ill.   II. Title.

PZ7.P3645 Mag 2010
[E]—dc22
                                                                2006051714